W is for Washington DC
Copyright © 2019 by Dry Climate Inc.

Printed in the United States

First edition

www.dryclimatestudios.com

ISBN
978-1-9424023-0-5

Library of Congress Control Number
2015900041

W is for Washington, DC

Written by Maria Kernahan
Illustrated by Michael Schafbuch with Mark Cesarik

A is for Air Force One, the White House in the sky.

Presidents still need to work even when they fly.

B is for the brass bands
that play on summer nights.

Concerts on the Capitol steps
are a musical delight.

C is for the Castle, the Smithsonian's first home.
Gothic and imposing, it's known for its red stone.

D is for the dogs that have lived in the East Wing.

Blackjack Roosevelt
Manchester Terrier

Liberty Ford
Golden Retriever

Calamity Jane Coolidge
Sheltie

Laddie Boy Harding
Airedale Terrier

Buddy Clinton
Chocolate Labrador Retriever

Le Beau Tyler
Italian Greyhound

Sebastian Monroe
Siberian Husky

Bo Obama
Portuguese Water Dog

Millie Bush
English Springer Spaniel

First families love them for the joy that they bring.

Rex Reagan
Cavalier King Charles Spaniel

Him & Her Johnson
Beagles

Heidi Eisenhower
Weimaraner

Buzzy Jefferson
Briard

Dot Hayes
Cocker Spaniel

Faithful Grant
Newfoundland

Blaze Roosevelt
Mastiff

Barney & Miss Beazley Bush
Scottish Terrier

Wolf Kennedy
Irish Wolfhound

E is for engravings
from which dollar bills are printed.

At the "money factory" US currency is minted.

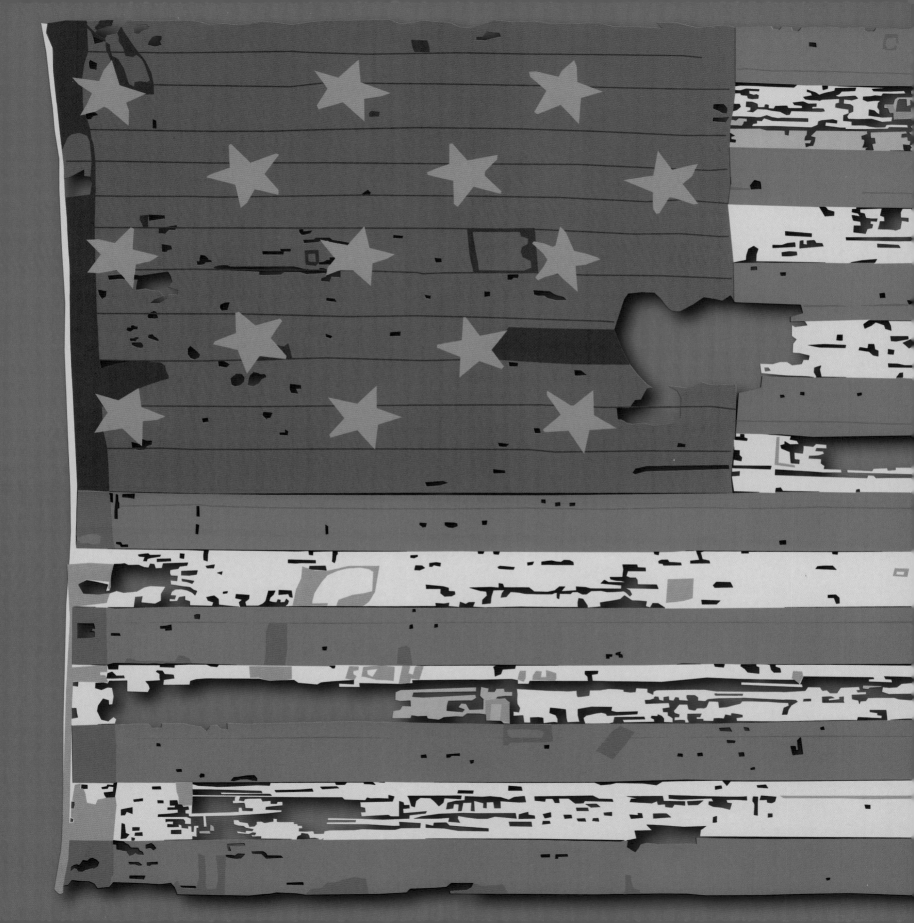

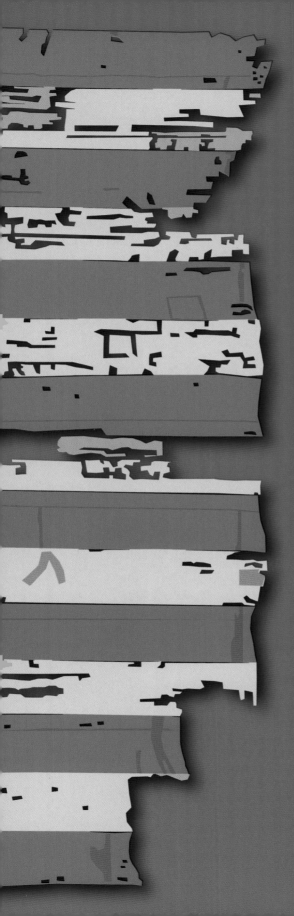

F is for the flag
that flew at early light.

The Star-Spangled Banner
was inspired by our fight.

G is for the gargoyles
perched on the National Cathedral.

Not just simply waterspouts,
they also ward off evil.

H is for hiking through an oasis in the city.

In every season you'll find Rock Creek Park so pretty.

I is for the ice rink
at the National Gallery of Art.

Can you make a figure 8?
Try it after dark!

J is for **jerseys**
of our favorite teams.

Each season we start fresh
with championship dreams.

K is for kayaking on a hot summer day.
From the mouth of the Potomac
to the Chesapeake Bay.

L is for the Library of Congress
where you can see the largest book.

The smallest one is also there
but you'll need a closer look.

"Old King Cole" is about the size
of the period at the end of this sentence.

"Bhutan: A Visual Odyssey Across
the Last Himalayan Kingdom"
is 5 feet wide and 7 feet tall.

M is for the Metro
that runs under the ground.

The arriving and departing trains make quite a rumbling sound.

N is for the
National Museum of Natural History.

How that elephant got inside
is still something of a mystery.

THE ARC OF THE MORAL UNIVERSE IS LONG, BUT IT BENDS TOWARD JUSTICE

O is for the Oval Office,
where POTUS gets work done.

It's the place for meetings, calls,
and sometimes lots of fun.

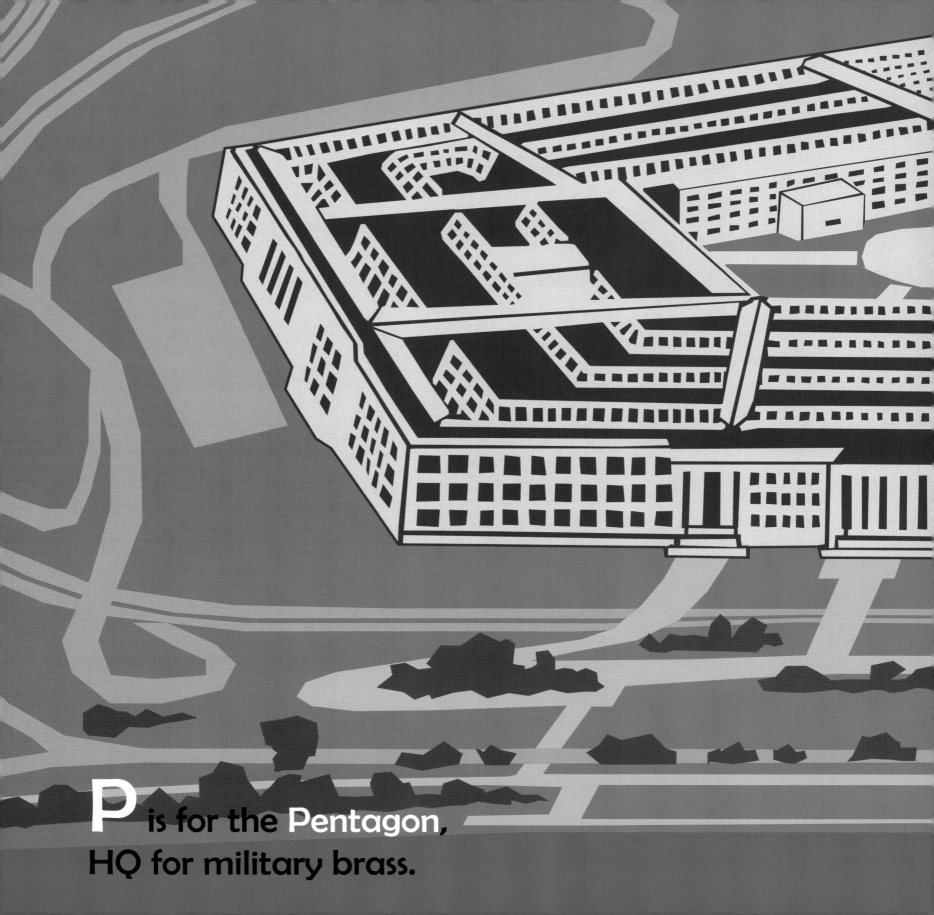

P is for the **Pentagon**,
HQ for military brass.

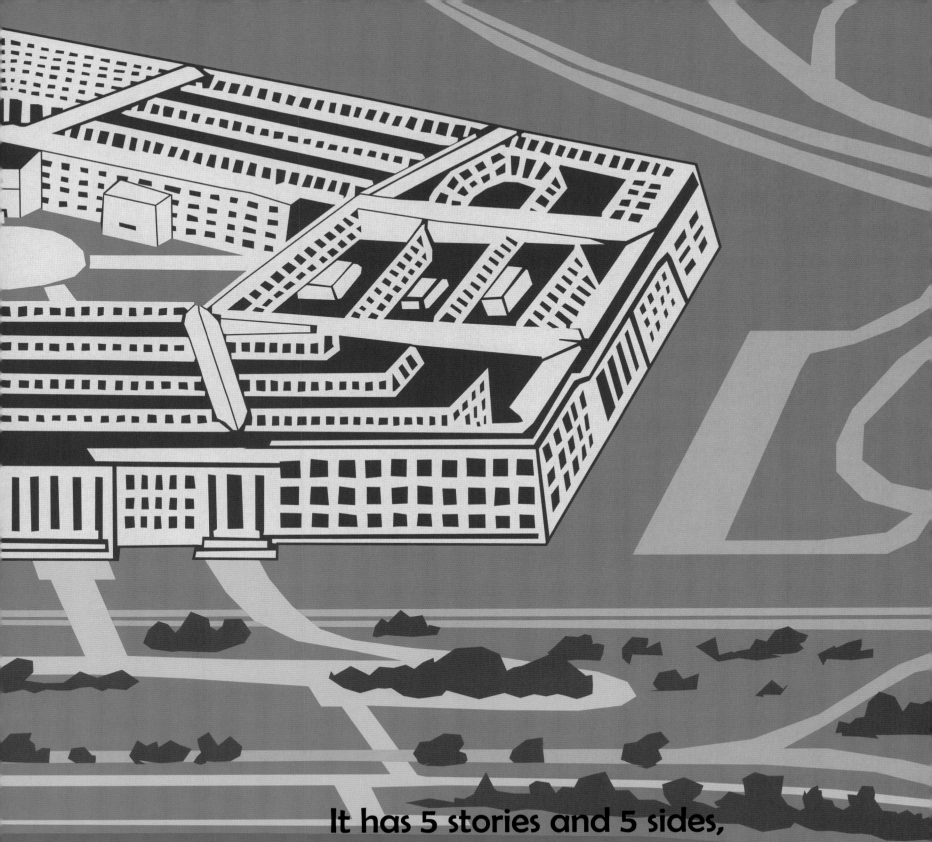

It has 5 stories and 5 sides,
plus a courtyard filled with grass.

Q is for the quotes by the Reverend Dr. King.

DARKNESS CANNOT DRIVE OUT DARKNESS, ONLY LIGHT CAN DO THAT. HATE CANNOT DRIVE OUT HATE, ONLY LOVE CAN DO THAT.

We honor his mission to let freedom ring.

R is for the Reflecting Pool on the National Mall.
In front of the Lincoln Memorial you will feel so small.

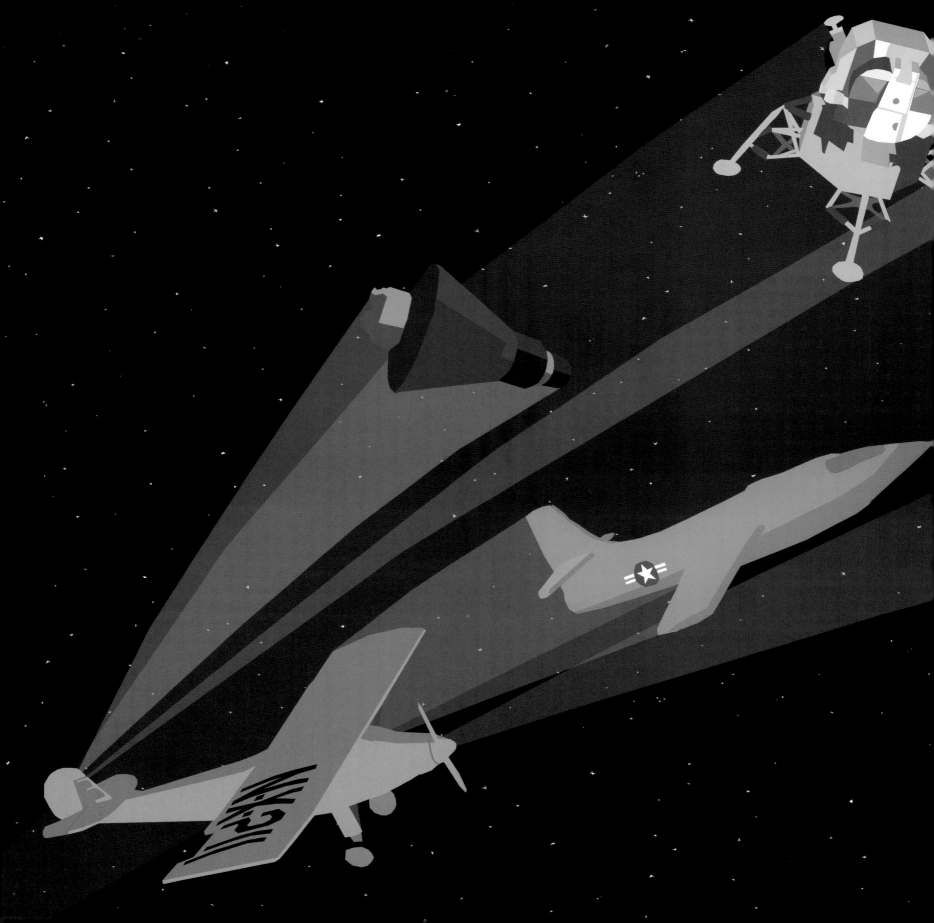

S is for the spacecraft
that rocketed in air.
At the Air and Space Museum
you will see them there.

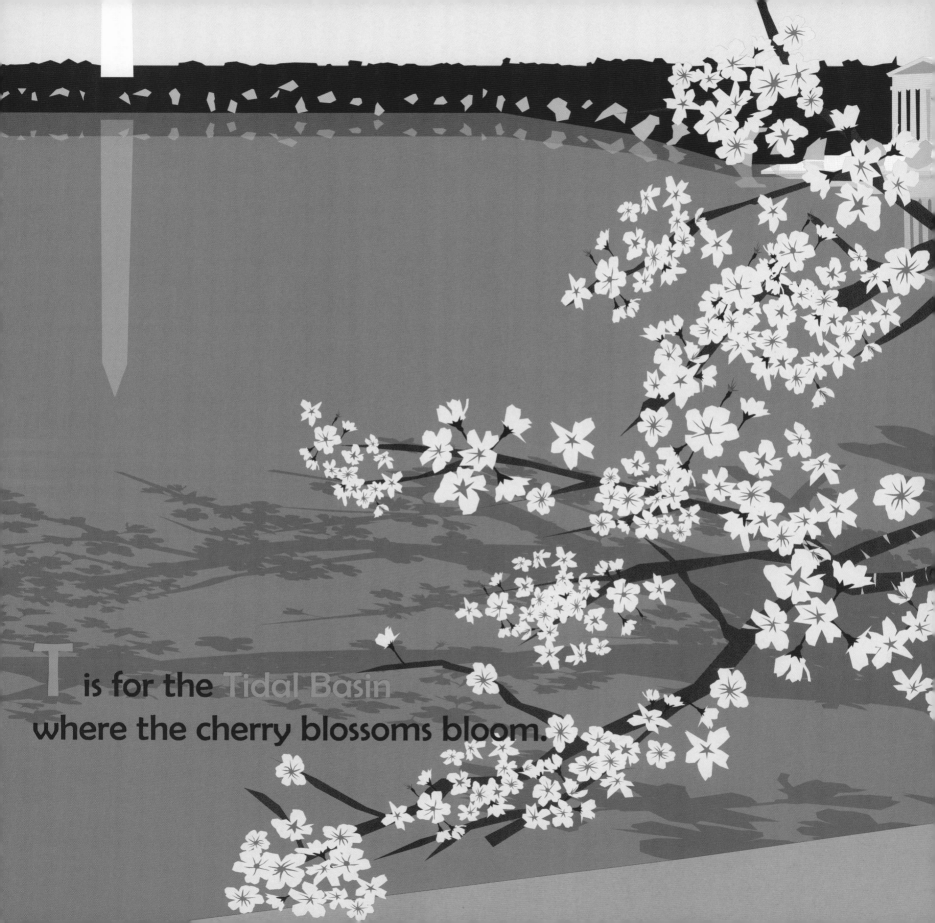

T is for the Tidal Basin
where the cherry blossoms bloom.

On a warm spring day
you can smell their sweet perfume.

U is for **Uncle Sam**, a symbol of this nation.
An icon in America, he's an historical creation.

V is for the valor
that our brave heroes displayed.

They fought for our country
even though they were afraid.

W is for the **White House**.
It's the home of the Presidents.

Abigail and John Adams were the first residents.

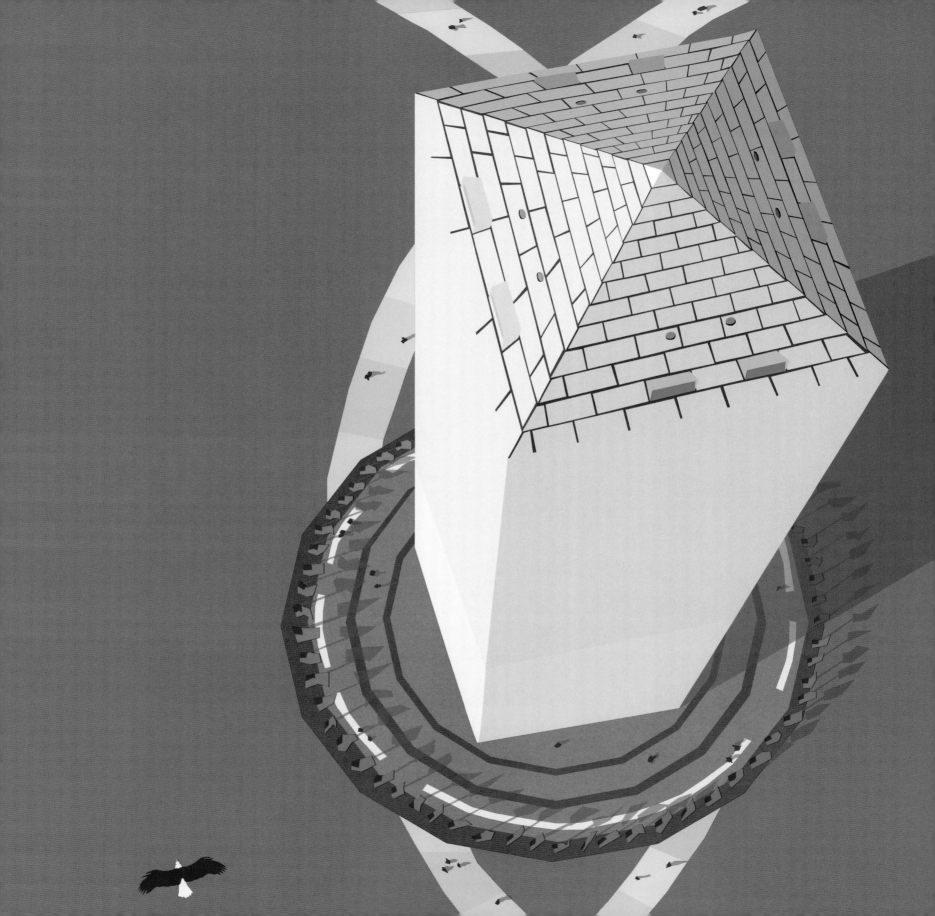

X is for the **X** at the highest point in town.
As you fly over, you'll see it looking down.

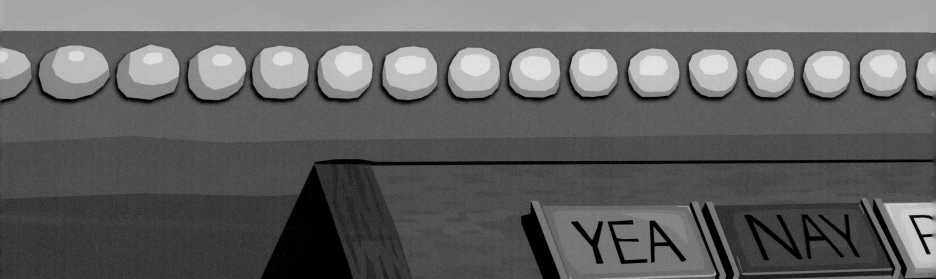

Y is for yea,
a vote that means yes.

Passing laws is the job
of the United States Congress.

Z is for National Zoo, where the pandas play.
Bison, bears and bobcats are also on display.

T is for Thank you, it's not just a letter.
Your help was amazing, it made us much better.

Christopher and Matthew, Meggie, Claire and Libby,
Maureen and Big Daddy.

Thanks to the folks who helped us along the way.
We need the extra eyes, big and little!

The Baumgarnters
Scott Hibbard
Judy Kernahan
The Levy-Howards
Abbie Littlejohn
Tara Magner
Chris Schafbuch
Mona Shin

A portion of the proceeds from this book
will be donated to literacy programs in
Washington, D.C. through DonorsChoose.org.

OTHER BOOKS IN THE ALPHABET SERIES FROM DRY CLIMATE STUDIOS:

FOR PRINTS, BOOKS AND GIFTS PLEASE VISIT
www.dryclimatestudios.com

DRY CLIMATE STUDIOS™